ELECTRIC CLAW

by Michael Dahl illustrated by Andy Catling

STONE ARCH BOOKS
a capstone imprint

Igor's Lab of Fear is published by Stone Arch Books
A Capstone Imprint
1710 Roe Crest Drive, North Mankato, Minnesota 56003
www.mycapstone.com

Cataloging-in-Publication Data is available at the Library of Congress
website.
ISBN 978-1-4965-3527-6 (library binding)
ISBN 978-1-4965-3531-3 (eBook PDF)

SEP   '16

SUMMARY: Two friends are playing video games at an arcade. Then
they turn their attention to the Claw. They realize the game is
rigged, but one boy doesn't want to go home without a prize. How
far will he go to get what he wants? And will his actions lead to
punishment?

COVER ILLUSTRATOR: Igor Šinkovek
DESIGNER: Kristi Carlson
EDITORS: Sean Tulien and Abby Colich

Printed in the United States of America in Stevens Point, Wisconsin.
009621F16

TABLE OF CONTENTS

Go away! There's no one here!

Take one more step and I'll lower the ceiling's spikes!

Oh. It's just you again.

Come in, my friend. Come in.

No, there aren't any spikes in
the ceiling.

I was simply playing a game on my
phone. That's all.

I see you're staring at my Claw trophy.

Lovely, isn't it? It's brand new.

It's great at, um . . . grabbing people's attention. Hehe.

And now that I've got yours, let me tell you a story . . .

CHAPTER ONE:
A NEW RECORD

Two boys aimed blasters at a large video screen.

"Ethan!" Grant said. "Watch out for that Martian bug-soldier!"

"I got it," Ethan said calmly.

They were playing in the Crazy Clown Arcade.

It sat a mile from town in an old mall.

Ethan sent one last blast at a space monster on the screen.

Lights **FLASHED**.

Sirens BLARED.

A message blinked on the video screen.

**YOU BROKE THE RECORD!
CONGRATULATIONS, ETHAN C.!**

"You did it!" Grant shouted. "You beat the high score!"

The other gamers in the arcade saw the lights and heard the noise.

Soon a crowd gathered around Ethan.

Ethan lowered the blaster. He slipped it into the holster.

"No big deal," Ethan said. "The last high score was mine too."

"Whatever," said Grant. "You're the best."

Ethan smiled.

CHAPTER TWO:
AN OLD GAME

The crowd parted. A boy no one knew stepped forward.

The boy smirked. "I bet you can't beat the Claw," he said.

"The Claw?" one girl said.

"What's that?" a boy said.

Ethan frowned. "I've never heard of it," he said.

The boy's eyes GLEAMED like silver.

"It's brand new. The Crazy Clown Arcade just got it in," he said.

"Think you can beat that too?"

Ethan shrugged. "I can beat any game here," he said.

"He's right," said Grant.

"Oh, yeah?" said the new kid. "Then prove it."

The boy led the crowd toward the back of the arcade.

In a dark corner sat a tall box with glass sides.

The box was filled with prizes. Toys, trinkets, and trophies were piled high.

In the center hung an enormous metal hand.

THE CLAW.

Ethan chuckled. "This game is old school," he said.

He stepped up and grabbed the joystick.

"Piece of cake," he said. "I'll give the prize to my girlfriend."

And he started to play.

CHAPTER THREE:
RIGGED

An hour passed.

Ethan still hadn't beaten the game.

About a hundred times, he had picked up a prize with the Claw.

And each time, the Claw dropped the prize.

The crowd was long gone. Even the new boy with the silver eyes had left.

Sweat shone on Ethan's forehead.

Grant looked **worried**.

"Come on, man," Grant said. "Let's get out of here. My grandma will kill me for being this late."

Ethan pounded on the glass box with his fist. "This stupid game is broken!" he snarled.

The sun had set 30 minutes ago. Now the inside of the Crazy Clown Arcade was all shadows.

It was dead silent except for the eerie hum of machines.

Grant **SHIVERED**. "Come on," Grant said. "This place is giving me the creeps."

"This game is rigged," Ethan grumbled. "That's why I couldn't beat it."

Grant nodded. "I know," he said.
"Can we go now?"

Ethan nodded. With that, the boys
left the arcade together.

They walked toward town beneath the moonless sky.

"Hey," said Grant. "Why did you say you'd give the prize to your girlfriend? You don't have a girlfriend."

Ethan shoved his hands in his pockets. "Shut up," he said. "You're embarrassing me."

Grant was going to point out that they were alone. Instead, he kept quiet.

They walked on in silence.

CHAPTER FOUR:
UP TO NO GOOD

Ethan clenched his jaw. His brain repeated a single thought over and over. *I deserve to win.*

"You okay, man?" Grant asked.

Ethan didn't answer.

When they reached a field, Grant waved goodbye. Ethan nodded. Then the boys went their separate ways toward their houses.

Ethan stopped. He listened to the wind **blowing** through the weeds. It sounded like whispers. Cold, squeaky whispers. It made him mad.

Ethan turned around and headed back to the Crazy Clown Arcade.

No lights were on in the arcade.
Ethan didn't see any employees
inside.

But the front door was unlocked.

He pulled open the door and
stepped inside. He headed for the
back of the arcade.

The Claw was **waiting** for him.

Ethan's eyes landed on one
particular prize.

A pink unicorn.

It would be the perfect gift for a girlfriend. That is, if he had one.

Ethan knew better than to keep playing the game.

The Claw <u>had</u> to be rigged.

So he knelt down. He shoved his hand into the box's prize chute.

His fingers grazed the arm of a **FUZZY** toy.

He grunted, pushing his arm farther inside.

Ethan reached for the toy.

"Ow!" Ethan cried.

The edge of the chute SLICED his finger.

Ethan didn't care.

He stretched his BLOODY fingers around
the pink unicorn. The machine creaked
under his weight.

He grabbed a hold of one of its pink ears. *"Yes!"* he said. He pulled the toy down the chute.

A second later, the prize was in his hands.

He looked down at the fuzzy toy.

One of the ears had blood on it.

Oh, well, thought Ethan. His fingers wrapped around the prize. I won. <u>That's all that matters.</u>

Ethan ran out of the arcade. Once outside, he turned to look back.

Above the entrance hung the giant clown's head.

Its big red smile seemed **WIDER** than normal.

He backed away. The clown's silver eyes seemed to follow his every move.

Ethan <u>*ran*</u>.

Soon he reached the field. He stopped to catch his breath.

The whispers were **LOuDeR** now. To Ethan, they sounded like squeaky hinges.

Ethan's eyes went wide. He looked up to see a giant metal claw descending on him.

The metal jaws grabbed him by his ankle. Ethan screamed as the Claw pulled him into the sky.

He looked down to see the field a thousand feet below.

Ethan was never seen again.

His friend Grant did find
something in the field.

A unicorn with a **BLOODY** ear.

Ethan always had to be the best.

But the Claw, well . . . the Claw had the upper hand.

Hehe. Heh Heh Heh Heh

PROFESSOR IGOR'S LAB NOTES

Do you like to play arcade games or other video games? Have you ever wondered how they work?

Video games and arcade games work like computers. They use technology called "user interface." User interface is how the game reacts when players make a move using a controller. Different computer games use different types of controllers. At the beginning of the story, the boys are playing a game that uses a blaster as a controller.

The user interface tells the video game screen what graphics to show. It also controls what sounds the game makes. The graphics and sounds coming from the game depend on what the player is doing to control it.

Are you interested in a career making video games? Considering learning more about computer science and graphic design. Skills in animation and story telling can also come in handy.

Just don't anger the Claw. Or you may become a part of the game rather than one of its creators!

GLOSSARY

ANIMATION (a-nuh-MAY-shuhn)—cartoons made by quickly presenting drawings, one after another, so that the characters seem to be moving

CHUTE (SHOOT)—a narrow pathway

CONTROLLER (kuhn-TROHL-uhr)—an input device used to play a video game

DESCEND (dee-SEND)—to move from a higher place to a lower place

EERIE (EER-ee)—strange, creepy, or mysterious

GRAPHIC (GRA-fik)—a visual image such as an illustration, photograph, or work of art

HOLSTER (HOHL-stur)—a holder for a gun

JOYSTICK (JOI-stik)—a stick that moves in the direction of the device it controls

RIG (RIG)—to fix something ahead of time so that the outcome is known

TECHNOLOGY (tek-NOL-uh-jee)—the use of science to do practical things, such as designing complex machines

DISCUSSION QUESTIONS

1. Who do you think the boy at the arcade with silver eyes is? Where else in the story are there silver eyes?

2. Do you think the Claw was rigged? Why or why not?

3. What happened to Ethan at the end of the story? Do you think what happened to him was fair punishment?

WRITING PROMPTS

1. On page 21 Ethan tells Grant he is embarrassed. Why do you think Ethan says he feels this way? Write about a time you felt embarrassed. Explain what happened.

2. At the end of story, Grant finds in the field the bloody unicorn that Professor Igor now has. Write another chapter to this story telling how Professor Igor gets the bloody unicorn from Grant.

3. Make up your own arcade game. Write about what it does and how it works.

AUTHOR BIOGRAPHY

Michael Dahl, the author of the Library of Doom, Dragonblood, and Troll Hunters series, has a long list of things he's afraid of: dark rooms, small rooms, damp rooms (all of which describe his writing area), storms, rabid squirrels, wet paper, raisins, flying in planes (especially taking off, cruising, and landing), and creepy dolls. He hopes that by writing about fear he will eventually be able to overcome his own. So far it isn't working. But he is afraid to stop, so he continues to write. He lives in a haunted house in Minneapolis, Minnesota.

ILLUSTRATOR BIOGRAPHY

Andy Catling is a professional scribbler and splurger of pictures and has illustrated for publishers around the world. He works in traditional mediums and digital wot-nots to make artwork with a rigorous mangle-like process. First he draws a picture. Then he rubs it out and draws it again. He colors using watercolor, pencils, and ink, sniffs it, screws it up, and starts over. The digital work process is much the same but without the sniffing. (All digital artwork smells of screen wipe.) Andy lives in the United Kingdom and thinks he is a pirate.